Pride Before a Fall
Thuli Marutle Leigh

Dedication

To the ones who carry unspoken stories in their chests —
the mothers who held the house together,
the fathers who meant well but did not know how to say it,
and the children who grew up in the middle of love and hurt.

May healing find you
in your own time.

Preface

Families are not broken all at once.
They are broken in small moments —
in the words that are not said,
in the apologies that come too late,
in the pride we mistake for strength.

This story was born from real life —
from households where love was present,
but tenderness was not always taught.
Where discipline spoke louder than affection,
and silence was the language of pain.

Pride Before a Fall is not written to judge,
but to understand.
It is a story of love that was real,
mistakes that were heavy,
and healing that arrived slowly —
sometimes only at the end.

If you have ever held regret in your chest,
if you have ever wished you could go back and
say the words you didn't say,
if you have ever loved someone but didn't know
how to show it —
this book is for you.

May it soften you.
May it remind you that connection is fragile.
And may it teach you, gently,
that love must be spoken while we still have time.

— Thuli Marutle Leigh

TABLE OF CONTENTS

Part One

The Breaking Point

Chapter 1: The Father Who Couldn't Bend

Mosa was a man shaped by discipline — and held together by pride.
He believed that order built character and that success came from doing things the right way. His father had raised him with a firm hand, and Mosa carried those lessons into every corner of his life.

He often said, "A tree bends when it's young — not when it's grown."
To him, punishment was not cruelty — it was correction, love expressed through firmness. He believed in corporal punishment and truly thought it was the only way to raise responsible children.

But Mosa's home was far from harsh. He was deeply loving — a husband who adored his wife and a father who cherished his children. He had built a beautiful life on his farm: wide golden fields, neat fences, loyal dogs,tractors that gleamed like trophies under the sun and pens filled with healthy pigs.The family lived comfortably, surrounded by laughter and routine.

His wife, Dimakatso, was elegance personified — beautiful, soft-spoken, and tidy to perfection. She filled their home with warmth and grace. The scent of her cooking and fresh flowers lingered in every room. The house was always spotless, her touch seen in every polished surface and carefully folded curtain.

Mosa loved her deeply, but he was not a man of many words — especially not the words "I'm sorry."
When he offended her, he didn't apologise directly. Instead, he found his own ways of making amends — a new bottle of her favourite cologne, or an expensive set of pots she had once admired. That was his language of remorse — silent, thoughtful, and wrapped in pride.

Together, they made a striking pair. People admired them — the disciplined man and the graceful woman, walking side by side through life with quiet confidence.

Their children, Bokang and Dineo, were their joy. Bokang was bold and curious, always asking questions and sometimes pushing boundaries. Dineo, gentle and imaginative, spent hours sketching or humming to herself.

Mosa was playful with them. He taught them to ride their fancy new bicycles down the dusty road, cheering loudly as they found their balance. But when they misbehaved, all it took was that look.

It wasn't a shout, nor a threat — just the heavy, wordless stare that said everything. The moment they saw it, their laughter froze. They knew the line had been crossed.

Mosa's love ran deep, but so did his need for order. He took pride in his home, in his wife, in his children, and in the man he had become. Pride made him strong, proud, and respected.

But pride also made him slow to yield.

And somewhere between his silence and his strength, his pride began to plant seeds that would one day bloom into heartbreak.

Chapter 2: The Lesson That Went Too Far

Weekdays in Mosa's house followed a rhythm: mornings smelled of steam and toast, Dimakatso's soft voice carried through the kitchen, and by seven o'clock both children were dressed in their neat uniforms. School was important to Mosa — it was the bridge from farm life to the wider world.

Of the two, Bokang was the one he pinned his highest hopes on.
Smart, quick to understand, the kind of boy who could solve his father's home trial tests in minutes. Mosa often said, "This one takes after me." He believed Bokang could go further than he ever had — university, perhaps even overseas. He believed in him that much.

But Bokang was a boy who didn't yet understand how precious that belief was.
He loved soccer more than study, sunshine more than sums. He lost his calculator, misplaced pens, tore pages from his notebook. Still, when his father gave him mock exams at home, he always came out with an A. That was what made it worse — Mosa knew what the boy could do.

The first time Bokang skipped school, he spent the day at the soccer field.
When Mosa found out, he called him aside quietly.
"Why were you not at school?"

Bokang's eyes darted. "I was late, Papa. Only two minutes. The gateman wouldn't let me in."

Mosa looked at him for a long moment, the way that froze the air in a room. He didn't raise his voice. "Next time, leave earlier," was all he said.

But the second time, the excuse didn't come so easily. When Mosa heard from the neighbour that the boy had been seen playing soccer again, he didn't wait for explanations. He walked to the shed, took Bokang's bicycle — the one the boy loved more than anything — and rode it down the dusty road to his brother's house. When he returned, his shirt was damp with sweat and his decision was firm.

"You will never see that bicycle again," he said simply.

Later that evening, he turned to Dineo. "And you
— don't even think of lending him yours. I know
the two of you; you'd trade the world for each
other. Not this time."

Dineo frowned, confused. "But, Papa, why not?
Where is his own bike even?"

"Ask your brother," Mosa replied, and that was the
end of it.

That night, the siblings sat on Dineo's bed in the
dim light of her bedside lamp.
She was younger, but wise for her years. "Bo," she
whispered, "why do you keep skipping? Papa's
really angry now."

Bokang sighed. "You won't understand."

"Try me."

He hesitated, then spoke, his voice small. "At
school... if you're late, even one minute, the
teacher hits you. Hard. So when I'm late, I just go
to the soccer field instead. Why should he beat
me like that? He's not my father."

"Has he hit you before?"

"Of course," Bokang said bitterly. "Why do you think I'd rather play soccer? He uses a stick, Dineo. I can't take that every morning."

Dineo's face softened. "Then tell Papa. He'll talk to him."

"I'd rather be in trouble with Papa than be called a snitch. One boy told on the teacher, and the man made his life hell until he changed schools. I won't go through that."

Dineo said nothing. She wanted to protect her brother, but she also wanted to protect him from their father's anger. That night she hardly slept.

A week later, the storm broke.

Bokang had missed school again — not once, but several times. The principal had called Mosa to the office and handed him a letter. The title at the top burned through him: Suspension Notice.

That evening, the family sat at dinner. Dimakatso was ladling stew when Mosa walked in, his boots still dusty from the road. He didn't greet. He didn't sit. He placed the letter flat on the table.

"Bokang. Read it."

The boy looked at it, confused. "What is — "

"I said read it."
The tone cut through the room.

Dimakatso froze, spoon mid-air. Dineo's eyes darted from her mother to her father.

Bokang read slowly, stumbling over the words, each one tightening Mosa's jaw.
When he finished, he stared at the floor.

Dimakatso took the letter gently from his hand. "Suspension letter?" she murmured, scanning it herself. Her breath caught.

Mosa's voice was calm, but it carried thunder beneath it. "You've been skipping school. Lying. Bringing shame to this house."

"Papa, I— "

"Enough!"

The table fell silent. Even the clock seemed to hold its breath.

"Dineo," Mosa said without looking at her, "go to your room."

"But — "

"Now."
The look came. The one that meant don't argue.

Dimakatso rose and guided the trembling girl down the hallway. At the doorway, she knelt to meet her daughter's eyes.
"Don't worry, baby," she whispered, pressing a kiss to her forehead. "We'll sort it out."

But before she reached the dining room again, a sound split the air — the sharp crack of a belt, followed by a cry.

"Mosa!" she shouted, running back.

Another strike. A louder scream.
The man who had once taught his son to ride a bike now stood in a storm of his own making — a father driven by disappointment, love, and pride twisted too tight.

Dimakatso froze in the doorway, her hands trembling, her voice lost between the urge to protect and the fear of making it worse.

Mosa's heart pounded with anger, but beneath it was something else — the deep, painful love of a father who wanted more for his child and didn't know another way to show it.

Outside, the night wind rose, pushing against the windows, echoing the chaos inside.

Chapter 3: The Breaking Point

Mosa had given his children long ropes all their lives.
He wasn't quick to punish; he always gave chances — warnings, talks, and more talks. When he finally resorted to the belt, it meant he had reached the edge of his patience. But this night... this one was different.

The sound of Bokang's cries still rang in his ears long after his arm grew tired.
He didn't even know how long it had gone on. The minutes blurred together — the belt, the shouting, the pleading. His anger had taken a shape of its own. It wasn't just about the suspension letter anymore — it was about every warning ignored, every lie, every broken rule.

When he finally stopped, his body felt heavy, his hands trembling.
He looked down. Bokang was on the floor, exhausted from screaming, tears drying on his cheeks, his small body limp and weak. The sight made something inside Mosa crack.

He glanced at the clock — nearly an hour had passed. His chest tightened.
In that moment, his eyes met Dimakatso's.

The look she gave him was one he would never forget.

It wasn't anger. It was disbelief — a mixture of pain and betrayal.

It said, How could you?

For the first time that night, Mosa felt something deeper than rage.

He felt shame. Regret. Fear.

But he didn't show it. He was a man — a man raised to hide emotion, to never appear weak. So, he turned and walked out of the house without a word.

As soon as the door closed, Dimakatso ran to Bokang, kneeling beside him. "My boy, my boy..." she whispered, helping him up. He was too weak to stand on his own. She guided him slowly to his room, laid him gently on the bed, pulled his blanket over him, and placed a pillow under his head.

"Are you okay?" she asked softly. "Do you think we need to take you to the hospital?"

Bokang shook his head, his voice faint. "No, Mama. I don't need a doctor. I'm in pain, but it's not that bad."

Dimakatso frowned, brushing the hair from his forehead. "Still, maybe tomorrow we should—"

"Mama," he said, his hand weakly holding hers. "Please don't be angry at Daddy. It's my fault. He warned me many times. I just didn't listen."

Dimakatso's eyes welled up. "I know, baby. We all make mistakes. It's not good to repeat them, but we are human. It happens. I love you."

"I love you too," he whispered.

She kissed his forehead. "Let me get you some painkillers."

He shook his head. "No, Mama. It's okay. I just want to sleep."

"Alright," she said softly. "Sleep, my boy."

She stood and walked out, closing the door halfway. Seconds later, Dineo crept in, her face pale and wet with tears.

"Bo," she whispered, running to him and hugging him gently.

He winced but smiled faintly. "It's okay, Dineo."

"I'm sorry," she said. "I told you to just tell Papa. Why didn't you?"

He sighed. "You saw him tonight. He didn't even give me a chance to speak. He was just... too angry."

"I've never seen him like that," she said quietly, sitting beside him. "He looked... different."

Outside, the night had turned cold.

Meanwhile, Mosa walked along the edge of the field, his boots crunching against dry soil. His hands were shaking, and his heart felt heavy. He had shed tears before, quietly, but this time they came harder, freely, as he walked in the dark.

He could still see the look in Dimakatso's eyes.
He could still see Bokang's small frame on the floor.

"What have I done?" he whispered into the night. "Mosa, what have you done?"

He thought of all the times he had laughed with Bokang — teaching him to ride his bicycle, watching him chase the dogs, joking about his crooked handwriting.
He thought about the promise he had made to himself — to be a better father than his own.

"Why did I let anger win?" he muttered. "He's my boy. My smart, stubborn boy."

He looked up at the stars and made a silent vow: I'll make it right.
Tomorrow, he would fetch the bicycle from his brother's house.
Tomorrow, he'd take Bokang to school himself, every day if he had to.
He would show him that love was louder than discipline.

"I'll make it right," he whispered again, wiping his tears. "I'll make it right."

Back in the house, Dineo stayed with Bokang until she began to drift in and out of sleep.
"Dineo," he murmured weakly, "can you get me some water? I'm so thirsty."

"Of course," she said, standing quickly. She looked at him for a moment — his skin looked pale, his breathing a little shallow — but she thought it was just exhaustion.

She fetched a glass of water, careful not to spill it, and brought it to his bedside.
"Here," she said softly.

Bokang lifted his head slightly and took a few sips. Then he smiled faintly, grateful. "Thank you," he whispered.

She was about to turn away when he burped softly, then exhaled — a long, uneven breath.

"Bo?" she said.

He didn't answer.

"Bo!" she said louder, shaking his arm.

The glass slipped from her hand and shattered on the floor.
"Mama!" she screamed.

Her cry pierced the night like lightning.

Outside, Mosa stopped mid-step.
The sound tore through him — it was a scream he
somehow knew too well.

His knees gave way. He fell to the ground, his
chest heaving, tears spilling down his face.

He didn't need to see.
He didn't need to ask.

He knew.

The boy he loved — the boy he wanted to save by
teaching, by correcting, by pushing — was gone.

And as the night swallowed his cries, Mosa
realized the terrible truth:
The lesson he had meant to teach had taken
everything from him.

Aftermath — The Night the House Went Silent

Dimakatso came running the second she heard
Dineo's scream.
Her heart pounded so fast she thought it might
burst.
She burst through Bokang's bedroom door,
almost slipping on the shattered glass scattered
across the floor.

"Bokang!" she cried, falling to her knees beside
the bed.
Dineo was already there, shaking her brother, her
tears falling fast.

"Mom, he's not waking up!" she sobbed. "I gave
him water — he just… he just…"

Dimakatso pressed her trembling hand to
Bokang's cheek.
It was cold. Too cold.
"Bokang, my boy!" she shouted, shaking him,
slapping his face gently. "Please, wake up!
Please!"

He didn't move.
He didn't breathe.

"No!" she screamed, gathering him in her arms, rocking him like he was still her baby. "Please, God, not like this!"

Dineo clung to her mother's side, sobbing uncontrollably, her tiny fingers gripping Bokang's sleeve.

Then Dimakatso said sharply, her voice shaking, "Dineo, go — go call the neighbours! Hurry!"

Dineo hesitated, terrified, frozen by what she was seeing.
"Mama, I—"

"Go!" Dimakatso shouted, her voice breaking. "Go now!"

Dineo ran.
She ran barefoot through the hallway, tears blurring her vision.
Her heart raced so fast she could barely breathe.

As she pushed open the front door, the night air hit her face. She stumbled forward, crying out for help. "Help! Somebody, please!"

And then — she saw him.

Just a few metres away, near the edge of the yard, Mosa was on the ground.
The man she had always seen as strong, tall, and unshakable — was on his knees, face buried in his hands, crying like a child.

His shoulders trembled with every breath. When he heard her voice, he looked up.
Their eyes met.

His face was wet with tears, his lips trembling.
"Dineo..." he whispered hoarsely, trying to stand, reaching out a hand toward her.

But Dineo froze. Her tears fell faster.
For the first time, she looked at her father not with love — but with fear.

He tried again, his voice cracking. "Dineo, come—"

She stepped back.
When he reached out to touch her hand, she pulled it away, shaking her head.

"Stay away," she whispered, her voice trembling. "Please."

Mosa's hand dropped slowly. His heart broke again — this time, in a way no punishment, no word, no apology could fix.

Dineo turned and ran into the darkness, screaming again for help as her small feet pounded against the dirt.

Behind her, Mosa stayed on the ground, his body shaking, his tears mixing with the dust.
He didn't follow her.
He couldn't.

He just whispered to himself, over and over, "I'll make it right... I'll make it right..." — but deep down, he already knew there was no "right" left to make.

Chapter 4: The Arrest

The flashing red lights broke the darkness first. The sirens wailed briefly, then fell silent, leaving only the hum of the police van and the low murmurs of neighbours gathering outside the gate.

Inside the house, Dimakatso sat on the floor beside Bokang's bed, holding his hand even though it was already growing cold. Dineo knelt quietly beside her, her small face blank and pale. The neighbours had called for help, and within minutes, the house was full of strangers — paramedics, police officers, and people whispering in disbelief.

The paramedics checked for a pulse, then looked at one another. One of them — a man with kind eyes — crouched near Dimakatso.
"Ma'am..." he said softly. "He's gone."

The words hit like a knife.
Dimakatso shook her head. "No... please, check again. He was just breathing a moment ago. Please."

The man glanced down, then shook his head gently. "I'm sorry."

That was the moment the world stopped moving. The hum of voices blurred, the flashing lights seemed to fade, and all she could hear was the sound of her own heartbeat.

They covered Bokang with a white sheet. Dimakatso reached out, clutching the edge of it. "Please," she whispered, "give me a moment."

The paramedics nodded and stepped back.

She leaned down and kissed her son's forehead through the sheet. "I love you, my boy," she whispered. "Sleep well."

When she stood, she turned — and there was Mosa, standing at the doorway, his face pale, his eyes hollow. He had been silent all this time, watching, trying to find words that didn't exist.

When the paramedics told him they needed to take the body to the mortuary, he stepped forward.
"Please," he said quietly. "Give me a moment with my son."

They nodded and left the room.

He knelt beside the small body, his hands trembling as he lifted the sheet to see Bokang's face one last time. His lips moved, but no words came. His heart was heavy with guilt, but his pride was heavier still.

"I didn't mean to," he whispered. "I swear, my boy, I didn't mean to."

Tears filled his eyes, falling silently onto Bokang's hand. He sat there for a long time, lost in the weight of what he'd done.

When they finally took the body, the sound of the stretcher wheels on the floor echoed like a drumbeat through the house. The door closed behind them, leaving silence again.

Dimakatso stood in the passage, watching them leave. Then, slowly, she turned and walked into the bedroom she once shared with Mosa. She opened the wardrobe and began to pack her clothes — calm, almost too calm.

"Mama," Dineo said quietly, standing at the door, "where are we going?"

Dimakatso folded a dress neatly. "To your grandmother's house.Go get your clothes ready too."

Dineo didn't argue. She looked relieved, as if she couldn't wait to leave. The man who was once her hero now scared her.

Dimakatso zipped the suitcase, her movements precise and deliberate, though her hands trembled slightly. On her way out, she paused by Bokang's room. The sight of the empty bed made her breath hitch.

She remembered his last words — "Mama, please don't be angry at Daddy."
A tear rolled down her cheek.

Just then, she felt a tap on her shoulder.
She turned — it was Mosa.

"Dimakatso," he said quietly, his voice shaking, "we need to talk about this."

She stared at him for a long moment. "Will it bring him back?"

He swallowed hard, his throat tight. "I didn't mean to—"

"You've said that already," she interrupted, her voice trembling but steady. "You didn't mean to. But you did. And now nothing will ever be the same."

He wanted to say I'm sorry.
He wanted to say it more than he had ever wanted to say anything in his life.
But the words stuck in his throat.
Sorry — such a small word, but one his pride had never allowed him to use.

Dimakatso looked at him, waiting — hoping.
But when nothing came, she turned away.

"Dineo, let's go," she said softly.

As they stepped out of the house, the sound of another vehicle approached. A police van pulled into the yard, its headlights bright against the dark.

Dimakatso stopped for a moment, clutching Dineo's hand.
She thought about staying — about helping Mosa explain — but the sight of the white sheet being loaded into the van earlier came back to her. The image of her son's face wouldn't leave her mind. She turned and walked toward the road.

Inside the house, the police moved quickly. One of them stepped forward.
"Mosa," he said firmly, "you're under arrest for the death of your son, Bokang Mosa."

Mosa's breath caught. "It was a mistake," he said. "I didn't mean to—"

"You can explain at the station," the officer interrupted. He pulled out the handcuffs.

When the cold metal locked around his wrists, something inside Mosa finally broke.
He didn't fight. He didn't speak. He just lowered his head as they guided him outside.

By now, the neighbours had gathered along the fence, their whispers thick with shock.
"Mosa?!" someone gasped. "No, it can't be!"

The officers opened the van and placed him inside. He sat quietly, staring down at his hands — the same hands that had once built his home, fixed his tractors, and taught his children how to ride their bikes.

As the van began to move, it turned onto the dirt road — and there, just ahead, stood Dimakatso and Dineo, waiting for a taxi.

Through the small back window, their eyes met.

For a moment, everything was still.

Mosa looked at them — his wife, his daughter — the only family he had left.
He wanted to speak, to say something, but all that came was a single tear that slipped down his cheek.

Dimakatso held Dineo's hand tighter.
Neither waved.
Neither spoke.

The van turned the corner, and Mosa disappeared from sight — leaving behind a house that had once been filled with love, now haunted by silence, sorrow, and the echo of pride.

PART TWO

The Years Of Distance

Chapter 5: The Funeral and the Sentence of the Soul

The courtroom was silent.
Only the faint echo of the ceiling fan filled the air as Mosa sat at the front, his hands folded, his eyes blank. He hadn't slept in days. His face looked pale, his once proud shoulders slouched.

His lawyer stood beside him, speaking softly to the judge. "Your Honour, this was not an act of hatred or cruelty. It was discipline gone too far. My client never intended to harm his son. He is a father who loved too deeply and punished too harshly."

The judge listened quietly, watching Mosa with tired eyes. He saw not a violent man, but a broken one — someone whose mind was trapped in the moment he wished he could undo.

When it was Mosa's turn to speak, he stood but said nothing. His lips moved, but no words came. His body was there, but his soul wasn't.

The judge sighed. "Mr. Mosa Kekana," he said gently, "there is no sentence heavier than the one you have already given yourself. You must live with what you have done, and that, I believe, will be punishment enough."

He paused, then added, "However, justice must still take its course. You will serve time. But for now, I will grant bail so that you may arrange your son's funeral and say goodbye properly."

Mosa nodded faintly. He didn't look up. As he left the courtroom, he asked his lawyer in a quiet, broken voice, "Did she come?"

The lawyer shook his head. "No, Mosa. I called her. She said she's mourning her son and wants no part of this."

Mosa's heart sank. He had hoped — foolishly — that Dimakatso would walk through the courtroom doors, that he could look at her one more time, that maybe she would see the regret in his eyes. But she hadn't come.

Outside, flashes of cameras caught his face as he stepped into the sunlight, but he didn't notice. His mind was far away — back at home, back in that small bedroom, back with the sound of his son's last words.

That evening, when he arrived home, the silence greeted him like an old friend.
The house was empty — the laughter gone, the walls cold. He walked through each room slowly, touching the furniture, the curtains, the photos on the wall. Every part of the house whispered a memory.

He sat down at the dining table where they had eaten every night — where Bokang used to steal pieces of bread before grace, and Dineo would giggle when Dimakatso scolded him.

He put his head in his hands and wept.
The sound echoed in the empty room, raw and unguarded — the sound of a man who had finally broken.

Later, he went into Bokang's room. The sheets were still neatly folded from the night Dimakatso had tucked him in. His schoolbooks lay stacked on the desk, one open to a half-finished maths exercise.

Mosa fell to his knees. "God, please," he whispered. "Please let this be a dream. Wake me up. I'll do anything — just wake me up. Yesterday, we were happy. Everything was fine. How did I lose it all in a few hours?"

But there was no answer. Only silence.

He stayed there for a long time, until the sound of people arriving broke through his thoughts. Neighbours, relatives, members of the community — all coming to pay their respects.

That night, the house filled with voices again, but it wasn't laughter this time. It was whispers, condolences, and the soft sound of crying. Mosa thanked everyone quietly, nodding, barely able to meet their eyes.

———

Two days later, the morning of the funeral arrived. The sky was grey — heavy, as if it too mourned the child gone too soon.

Mosa dressed slowly in a black suit. His hands trembled as he buttoned the shirt, the same hands that had once guided Bokang's small fingers on a bicycle handle.

He stood by the coffin, staring at it in disbelief. It felt unreal.
He kept glancing toward the gate, hoping — praying — that Dimakatso and Dineo would come.

But the service began, and the pastor's voice rose over the quiet sobs of the mourners. Still, there was no sign of them.

And then, just as the pastor began to speak about forgiveness, a car pulled up.
Every head turned.

It was Dimakatso, dressed in black, her face hidden behind dark glasses. Beside her was Dineo, holding her grandmother's hand. Behind them walked other relatives, solemn and quiet.

Mosa's heart ached at the sight. He wanted to run to them, to fall at their feet, to say the words that had been trapped in his chest for days — I'm sorry.

But he couldn't.
He just stood there, frozen, watching them take their seats beside his family without looking at him.

For Mosa, that moment felt like a final goodbye — not just to his son, but to the life he once had.

When the pastor called the family forward to view the body, Dimakatso held Dineo's hand tightly. They walked to the coffin together, silent, strong, and broken. Dimakatso's hand trembled as she brushed Bokang's cheek one last time.

Mosa stood behind them, his chest burning, wanting to say something — anything.
He took one small step forward, then stopped.

His throat tightened.
The words were right there.
But pride — that same pride that had built him, shaped him, and destroyed him — held his tongue once again.

He wanted to say, "I'm sorry."
But all that came out was silence.

As the coffin was lowered into the ground, Mosa felt something inside him sink with it.
The pastor prayed, the crowd wept, and the wind carried the sound of the soil falling — one handful at a time.

When it was over, Dimakatso turned and walked away, Dineo's hand in hers. She didn't look back. And Mosa, surrounded by people, had never felt more alone.

Chapter 6: An Empty House

When Mosa returned home after the funeral, the house was full—but he had never felt lonelier. Relatives moved about the rooms, talking softly, offering comfort that sounded hollow. To him they were kind faces, yes, but strangers. The only people he wanted to see—Dimakatso, Dineo, and Bokang—were gone. One by choice. One forever.

As the days passed, the visits slowed. The murmurs of sympathy faded.
Soon the footsteps stopped altogether, and the once-busy home sank back into silence.
It was just Mosa now, alone with the echo of what had been.

He spent hours staring at the doorway, half-expecting to see Dineo's small frame rushing in, or Dimakatso calling him to eat. The air still held her perfume, faint and heartbreaking.
Every room carried a memory, and every memory felt like punishment.

The summons back to court came sooner than he expected.

When the guards led him inside, the benches were half-filled with curious faces and reporters. The judge read the charges again—culpable homicide, the death of his own child.

His lawyer spoke quietly, asking for mercy. "Your Honour, he never intended this. He is a man destroyed by his own hands. There is no sentence harsher than the one he will serve inside himself."

Mosa kept his head down. He didn't try to defend himself. No one needed to tell the judge he was sorry; anyone looking at him could see it.

When the judge finally spoke, his tone was solemn. "Fourteen years. It should be life, but there is remorse here that the law cannot measure."

Mosa looked around the courtroom again— hoping, searching—for Dimakatso, for Dineo. The seats were empty.

That same morning, miles away, Dimakatso lay in bed with the curtains drawn.
She knew what day it was. The lawyer had called earlier to say sentencing was taking place.
But she didn't want to hear details; she was still learning to breathe through the weight of grief.

She spent most days asleep or staring at nothing.
Her body moved, but her spirit felt buried with her son.

Dineo tried to stay close to her mother, though she carried her own heavy burden.
Sometimes, in the quiet, she saw her brother's face—the way he had asked for water that night.

"Maybe I shouldn't have given it to him," she whispered once.
Dimakatso turned to her quickly. "No, baby. Don't ever think that."
But the guilt had already taken root.

That same day, Dineo made a promise to herself: I'll become a nurse. One day I'll know how to save people. Maybe then I'll forgive myself.

She avoided speaking about her father.
But deep down, she carried both anger and love—
a confused mix she couldn't untangle.
She was angry that he hadn't come for them, that
he hadn't said sorry.
Yet she could never forget the look on his face
that night—the tears she had seen when she ran
outside for help.

Somewhere in her small, aching heart, she knew
he was sorry.
But knowing it wasn't the same as hearing it.

And so the years began—years that stretched like
a long, empty road between a broken man and
the family he had lost.

Chapter 7: Letters Never Sent

Prison was quiet — too quiet.
The kind of quiet that made a man hear his own guilt.

Days blurred into weeks, and weeks into years. The walls were grey, the food tasteless, and the silence louder than any punishment the court could give. But Mosa didn't complain. He worked in the garden, cleaned the hallways, kept to himself. The guards said he was one of the "good ones." But if they had looked closer, they would've seen that the quiet wasn't goodness — it was grief.

Every night, he sat on his thin bed, a small notebook balanced on his knees. That's where he wrote his letters — to Dimakatso and to Dineo.

My dearest wife...
My little girl...

Page after page, he poured his heart out — confessions, regrets, and the word he could never say aloud: sorry. He wrote it again and again, as if one day the letters would somehow find their way to them.

But every time he finished, he folded the page, pressed it flat, and tucked it under his mattress.
Not yet, he told himself.
Not until I can face them.

Back home, Dimakatso was learning to live again — or at least, to pretend to.

She still had nights when sleep refused to come, when she'd wake up thinking she'd heard Bokang's laughter echoing down the hallway. The house felt too small for grief, too full of memories.

Yet she made herself get up every morning. She cooked, she cleaned, she smiled for Dineo — because Dineo needed her to.

Her daughter was her reason now.

Dineo had changed. She no longer giggled the way she used to, but she carried herself with quiet determination. Her grades improved, her focus sharpened, and the day she told her mother she wanted to be a nurse, Dimakatso cried for the first time in months.

"I just want to help people, Mama," Dineo said softly. "Maybe if I knew better that night... maybe Bokang—"

Dimakatso stopped her gently. "No, baby. Don't do that to yourself. You were a child. You did nothing wrong."

But deep down, both of them still lived in that night.

Six years later, Mosa was released on good behaviour.

The judge's words from long ago had been true — there was no sentence harsher than living with what he had done.

He walked out of prison thinner, quieter, older. He went straight home to the farm, but the silence there was heavier than the prison walls had ever been.

He still had all his letters — each one neatly stacked, yellowed by time. Sometimes he read them aloud to himself, imagining his wife's soft voice answering, imagining Dineo's laughter on the other end.

He told himself he would send them soon.

But soon never came.

A few times, he drove all the way to Dimakatso's mother's house. He knew the road by heart now. He would park a few meters from the gate, his heart pounding, his hands shaking. The bundle of letters lay on the seat beside him.

But when he looked at that gate — the gate that separated him from everything he had lost — he couldn't move.
What would he even say if she came out?
How could he ever look his daughter in the eye?

He would sit there for a while, then turn around and drive home, whispering, "Next time. Next time, I'll do it."

One morning, he woke earlier than usual.
Something in him said, Go now.

He drove to the same corner and parked where he always did.
Then, through the half-open gate, he saw them.

Dineo, wearing a crisp white nurse's uniform, her hair neatly tied back.
Dimakatso, radiant and graceful, helping her daughter adjust the collar, her hands gentle and proud.

He had heard from neighbours that it was Dineo's first day at university, and now he was seeing it with his own eyes. His heart twisted — pride and sorrow mixing painfully inside him.

He watched as Dimakatso brushed something off Dineo's shoulder and smiled, whispering something that made her daughter laugh softly.

Dineo turned to leave, walking tall, confident — her mother's daughter in every way.

For a brief second, she looked toward the street — toward Mosa's car. Their eyes didn't meet, but she paused, frowning.

"Was that…?" she whispered to herself. "No. It can't be. Forget it, Dineo. It's your first day. Let's do this for Bokang."

She straightened her shoulders, lifted her chin the way her mother always taught her, and walked off toward the taxi stop.

Mosa, heart pounding, quickly started the car and drove away. His hands shook on the steering wheel. He told himself it was enough — just seeing her alive, strong, and smiling. But deep down, he wanted more.

He wanted his family back.

———

That same morning, Dimakatso's mother asked quietly, "Did you hear? They say Mosa's been released on good behaviour ."

Dimakatso didn't look up from tying her shoes. "He never had bad behaviour," she said softly. "So that's to be expected."

Her mother hesitated. "Do you think you'll go and see him?"

"For what?" she replied flatly. "Who needs to apologise between us?"

Her mother sighed. "He's still your husband."

Dimakatso let out a small, humourless laugh. "He's many things, Mama. But sorry has never been one of them."

Her mother looked at her for a long moment. "What if he comes here?"

Dimakatso laughed again — a real laugh this time, shaking her head. "That would be a miracle."

She kissed her mother on the cheek. "Don't worry yourself, Mama. Some doors, once closed, shouldn't be reopened."

She picked up her handbag, straightened her blouse, and walked out — graceful, strong, and heartbreakingly composed.

Back on the farm, Mosa sat on the porch with the morning light on his face, a cup of cold tea beside him, and a pile of unsent letters on his lap.

He opened the first one and read it again — quietly, to no one.

My dearest Dimakatso,
If I could turn back time, I would give anything just to hear your laughter in this house again.
Tell Dineo I see her everywhere I go.
Tell her I'm proud. Tell her… I'm sorry.

He closed the letter carefully and placed it back in the pile.
Then he looked toward the empty road leading away from the farm.

The road where his family had once left him behind.
The road he still hoped, one day, they might return from.

Chapter 8: The Woman Who Looked Like Her

The farm still stood tall and beautiful, but it
wasn't the same.
Nothing was.

The grass grew wild, the flowers Dimakatso had
once planted had faded, and the air that used to
carry laughter now held only wind.

When Mosa went to prison, he had left his pigs in
his brother's care — strong, healthy animals he
had once been so proud of. They had multiplied
over the years, and when he returned, his brother
handed the farm back in good condition. But even
with the animals still there, it felt... different.

They no longer came running when he called.
They didn't squeal or play the way they used to
when Bokang threw feed into their pen and
laughed as they fought over it. Everything
seemed quieter now, as if even the animals could
sense what was missing.

Mosa had money, land, and comfort — but not
peace.
Because wealth couldn't fill the spaces where
love used to live.

Every morning he woke to silence. He would make his tea, walk the land, check on the tractors, feed the pigs, and return home to nothing but the hum of his own thoughts.

He still cleaned the house the way Dimakatso liked it — curtains washed, windows shining — as though she and Dineo might walk in any minute and say, "We're home."

One afternoon, he drove into town for groceries. The mall was bright and full of noise — a sound he hadn't heard in years. As he walked past the perfume counter, he caught a familiar scent — the same kind Dimakatso used to wear.

He turned sharply, and there she was.
Same build. Same walk. Same grace.

"Dima..." he whispered, his heart leaping.

He followed her through the aisle, moving faster when she turned a corner. She disappeared for a moment behind a group of shoppers, and he broke into a half-run.

When he finally reached her, he tapped her shoulder gently.
"Dima—"

The woman turned.

She wasn't Dimakatso.
Her eyes were kind, her face warm — but she wasn't her.

Mosa froze, embarrassed. "Pardon me," he said softly. "I thought you were someone I know."

She smiled, amused. "No problem."
Then she walked away, disappearing into the crowd.

Yet something stirred inside him.
For the first time in years, he felt… alive.

He went home that day and cleaned the entire house — the kitchen, the rooms, the porch. He polished the table they once ate at, washed the curtains, trimmed the grass. He even dusted Bokang's old bicycle, still leaning quietly in the corner.

He told himself he was preparing for something. Maybe even for them to come back.

And from that day on, he went to that same mall every morning — pretending to shop, hoping to see her again.

Yet something stirred inside him.
For the first time in years, he felt... alive.

He went home that day and cleaned the entire house — the kitchen, the rooms, the porch.
He polished the table they once ate at, washed the curtains, and trimmed the grass until the smell of cut leaves filled the air.

He even dusted Bokang's old bicycle, which he had asked his brother to bring back to the farm, still leaning quietly in the corner beside Dineo's smaller one. The sight of them together — still, untouched, side by side — made his heart twist.

Inside the house, he walked slowly from room to room. On every wall hung pieces of the life they had built together: wedding photos, family portraits, Bokang holding his first piglet, Dineo sitting on her father's shoulders, Dimakatso laughing in her Sunday dress.

Mosa stood staring at them for a long time. Then, one by one, he took them down.
He wrapped each frame carefully in cloth and placed them inside a wooden box.

He tucked the box away in the back of his wardrobe — somewhere only he would know.

That's where he kept everything he could not let go of:
the family pictures,
the letters he had written from prison but never sent,
and his marriage certificate to Dimakatso — proof of a love that, despite everything, neither of them had ever undone.

Every now and then, when the silence grew too loud, he would open that box.
He would read the letters, trace her signature on the certificate, and look at the faces smiling back at him from a world that no longer existed.

Then he would close the box again, hide it away, and whisper into the quiet,
"Maybe one day... maybe they'll come home."

He told himself he was preparing for something. Maybe even for them to come back.

And from that day on, he went to that same mall every morning — pretending to shop, hoping to see her again.

———

Weeks passed before he did.

He was in the parking lot, returning his trolley,
when a voice behind him said,
"Excuse me, sir — you forgot your wallet."

He turned.
It was her — the same woman he'd mistaken for
Dimakatso.

This time, they both laughed at the coincidence.

"I keep running into you," he said.

"Maybe it's fate," she teased. "I'm Lerato."

He nodded. "Mosa."

They talked for a while — about little things at
first. The weather. The price of vegetables. Life in
the countryside. Her laughter was soft, and when
she smiled, something warm spread through him
— a feeling he hadn't known in years.

Soon, they began to meet often — sometimes by
chance, sometimes by quiet arrangement. She
would help him pick out groceries, bring small
gifts for the farm, and listen when he spoke about
simple things.

He didn't tell her much about his past.
And she never pressed.

What drew him in wasn't just her kindness — it
was how much she reminded him of Dimakatso.
Her gentle nature, her warmth, even her perfume.
The resemblance was uncanny, almost cruel.

He told himself it wasn't love — just comfort.
But deep down, he knew she was filling the space
his grief had carved out.

Months passed, and Lerato became part of his
routine — the sound of her voice breaking the
stillness of his days.
She was kind, gentle, and patient, never truly
understanding the storm that lived inside him.

Then one evening, she stood by the doorway, her
hands trembling with excitement.

"Mosa," she said softly, "I'm pregnant."

For the first time in years, he smiled — a real smile that reached his eyes.
He placed his hand on her stomach.

"It's a boy," he said quietly. "And I already know his name."

"What name?"

He looked away, blinking back tears. "Bokang."

She smiled. "That's beautiful."

He nodded. "Yes... it is."

But only he knew the pain behind it.

After their son was born, Lerato began asking about marriage.
"We've built a life together," she said one night. "We should make it right."

Mosa looked away. "Soon," he said.

But soon never came.
Because in his heart, Mosa knew the truth — he was still married to Dimakatso.
And even if she never returned, he would never divorce her.

Two years later, Lerato became pregnant again. By now the neighbours knew her well — kind, polite, always helping others — but gossip found its way through the quiet streets.

One day, while Lerato bought vegetables at the same market where they'd first met, an older woman leaned closer and whispered, "My dear, you seem lovely, so I'll tell you the truth. That man you live with — he has a wife. A real wife. He never divorced her."

Lerato froze.
That evening, she waited for Mosa to return.

"They say you're married," she said quietly.

He sighed and rubbed his forehead. "Yes... but it's over."

"Then end it," she said firmly. "Either you divorce her and marry me, or I won't keep this baby."

Mosa hesitated. He couldn't lose another child. He told her he had met with a lawyer, that the divorce process had begun, and that they would have a traditional ceremony in the meantime.

Lerato's eyes filled with relief. "Really?"

He nodded. "Yes. Soon."

When the baby came, it was a girl.
Mosa held her in his arms, his heart trembling.

"What shall we name her?" Lerato asked softly.

"Dineo," he whispered.

Lerato smiled. "That's beautiful."

He kissed the baby's forehead and closed his
eyes.

Because once again, he wasn't naming new
children.
He was naming memories.
Chasing ghosts.
Trying to rebuild a home that no longer existed.

Part Three

The Last Chance

Chapter 9: The Woman Who Couldn't Reach Him

The day of the wedding dawned bright and loud.
Drums, laughter, and the hum of guests filled the air around Mosa's farmhouse.
For the first time in years, the place looked alive again.
Colourful tents covered the yard, women stirred pots, and men carried chairs and drinks.

Mosa and Lerato were having their traditional wedding—a celebration Lerato had long insisted on after their second baby was born.

Relatives, friends, and neighbours gathered in numbers; everyone wanted to witness the wedding of the popular farmer who, despite the shadows around his name, still commanded quiet respect.

When the time came to exchange vows, Lerato smiled brightly, her voice trembling with joy.

"I thank God for this day," she said, "and for the two precious gifts He gave us—our children, Bokang and Dineo."

A murmur rippled through the crowd.
Heads turned, whispers spread like fire.
The pastor had to raise his hand and call
everyone to order before continuing.

Lerato stood frozen for a moment, confused.
Had she said something wrong?

Mosa knew.
He heard every whisper, saw every sideways
glance.
But he kept his face calm, his eyes distant,
pretending not to notice.
He just wanted the ceremony over—wanted
Lerato off his back, the noise gone, the day
finished.

After the ceremony, while guests were eating,
Lerato's mother called her aside.

"What is this I'm hearing?" she asked sharply.

Lerato frowned. "About what, Mama?"

"Don't play with me, Lerato. Why on earth would you allow Mosa to name your children after the ones from his previous marriage? And worse—why would you marry a man who isn't divorced? You've humiliated us! The whole family!"

Lerato's heart dropped. "What? No, Mama, that can't be true—he said—"

Her mother shook her head in disgust. "You've shamed us today. Fix it."
Then she turned and walked away. One by one, her relatives followed, leaving Lerato standing alone amid the laughter of strangers.

Humiliation burned through her. She went inside, shut the door, and fell on the bed, sobbing until her head ached.
Something inside her whispered, There's more to this man than you know.

She wiped her tears and began to search.

She opened drawers, pulled clothes from hangers, and searched through cupboards. When she reached the last wardrobe, she noticed a small compartment high up—so high she had to climb onto a chair to reach it.

There, tucked neatly away, was a wooden box.

Her hands shook as she opened it.
Inside were family pictures, old letters, and a
marriage certificate.

The photos showed Mosa with another woman
and two children—a boy and a girl.
Their faces glowed with happiness, captured in a
time before tragedy.

She picked up the certificate, reading the name
aloud in a whisper.
"Dimakatso…"

Her heart sank.

Just then, the door opened.
Mosa froze at the sight—Lerato holding the
marriage certificate in her trembling hands.

In an instant, he rushed forward, snatching it
away from her grasp. His voice cracked, trembling
with fury and fear.

"Don't ever—ever—go through my things!"

Lerato stared at him, stunned.
He was shaking, clutching the certificate to his
chest as if it were life itself.

She had never seen him like that.
Not angry. Not violent. But... desperate.

He grabbed the rest of the letters from the bed,
threw them into the box, and stormed out of the
house.
The sound of his car engine faded down the road,
leaving Lerato alone, speechless.

———

Mosa drove straight to his lawyer's office.
He didn't trust anyone now—not even himself. He
wanted the box kept somewhere safe, away from
curious eyes.

When he arrived, the lawyer was startled to see
him carrying a sealed package.

"Keep this for me," Mosa said. "Lock it up. Don't
open it."

The lawyer nodded, placing it in the cabinet.
Then, hesitating, he said,
"By the way, a woman called earlier—Lerato. She
asked about a divorce case.

Mosa's head snapped up. "What did you say to her?"

"I told her there isn't one—'Divorce? What divorce?' "

Mosa sighed heavily. "Next time, just say it's still in process."

The lawyer frowned. "Then you should tell me next time before you lie about it."

Mosa didn't answer. He just nodded and left.

―――

Back home, Lerato was waiting for him, her eyes red and swollen.

"Can you explain yourself before I leave?" she said. "Who are Bokang and Dineo that you named my children after? And why would you lie about divorcing your wife?"

"I am divorcing her," he snapped.

"Oh really?" she shot back. "That's good—because I have Dimakatso's number."

His face changed instantly. "Don't you dare."

Lerato stepped back. She had never seen him like that—cold, fierce, protective.
"Oh, so you do care," she said quietly. "You'll never divorce her, will you?"

Without thinking, Mosa shouted, "No, I won't! You can stay or you can leave—but if you leave, you leave Bokang and Dineo here!"

The words hit her like a slap.

Tears welled in her eyes. "You don't love me," she whispered. "You've never loved me."

She stormed out, slamming the door.

Meanwhile, across town, at her workplace clinic, Dimakatso was tying her hair back from her face when her aunt walked in with a small, careful voice.

"Have you heard?"

"Heard what?" Dimakatso asked, not looking up.

"Mosa... he got married today. To that woman he stays with now."

The room became silent.

Dimakatso nodded once. Slowly.

"Oh. Okay. That's... fine."

She even smiled — the kind of smile that hurts the bones of the face.

She continued arranging the medication trays like nothing was wrong, but something inside her shifted.

But the news did not leave her.
It sat in her chest like a stone.

We are not even divorced.
He couldn't even speak to me.
Not even once.
He couldn't close our chapter.
He never apologized.

Her hands began to tremble.

And then, the memories began — flooding faster
than she could swallow them:

Their days of joy:
Mosa walking to the tractors while she watched
him from the kitchen window.
His kiss on her cheek when he came in smelling of
soil and sunlight.
Bokang learning to ride his bicycle — Mosa
steadying him with both hands.
Dineo running through the yard, laughing.
Evenings full of warmth, food, and home.

Then, the night of the breaking:
The belt.
The screams.
Her voice begging.
Dineo running for help barefoot.
The moment Bokang stopped crying.
The silence that followed — heavier than death itself.

Then, the police van:
Mosa sitting in the back of the van, tears streaming down his face.
And then she — froze— unable to move, unable to breathe, unable to forgive.

She still loved him.
After everything.
She didn't know how to stop.

That was the wound.
That was the pain.
Love that had nowhere left to go.

Her heart squeezed sharply — as if it had been struck from inside.

She pressed her hand to her chest.

One breath.
Another.
Pain radiating down her arm.
Her vision blurring at the edges.

The tray slipped from her hands and clattered onto the floor.

She tried to say something — her lips parted — but no sound came.

Her knees buckled.
She clutched her heart — right over it — fingers trembling.

And then she fell.

Her coworkers rushed to her side, calling her name, calling for help, calling for air, calling for time—
but time had already left.

Her pulse was gone before they touched her.

She died there on the clinic floor — not from hatred, not from anger — but from a heart that broke while still loving him.

Mosa sat down heavily, trying to steady his breathing.
The box was gone now — locked away safely where Lerato could never touch it.

He picked up his phone to call his lawyer — but before he could dial, it rang.

He answered with a tired sigh.

On the other end was Dimakatso's uncle, his voice thin, strained, almost breaking.

"Mosa… listen to me. I don't know how to say this… but Dimakatso collapsed at work today. They tried to help her, but… she didn't make it."

The phone slipped from his hand and hit the floor.

For a long moment, the world made no sound at all.
No air.
No thought.
Just silence.

Mosa's eyes stared into nothing — and everything came rushing back:

Her laughter in the kitchen.
Her perfume on Sunday mornings.
Her smile when she looked at him from the
window while he crossed the yard.
Bokang learning to ride his bicycle.
Little Dineo holding both their hands.
The night everything broke.
And the police van door closing.

His heart did not beat — it ached.

He didn't cry.
He couldn't.

He simply sat there, unmoving, as though grief
had turned him to stone.

Lerato returned from her walk and found the
house eerily quiet.
She walked into the bedroom, gathered her
things, folded the children's clothes, and packed
their bags.
She did not rush — she moved slowly, like
someone who already knew how the story ended.

The children stood beside her, small hands holding onto her dress.

When she finished, she walked back into the living room.

Mosa was still sitting in the same chair, the phone lying beside him.
His hands were open in his lap.
His eyes were empty — not angry, not cold, just... gone.

Lerato paused — the weight of the moment pressing into her chest.
She wanted to say something.
Anything.

But there was nothing left to say.

She walked past him without a word.
The children followed.

Mosa looked up at them — slowly — as though waking from a dream.

His eyes met theirs.

He wanted to speak.
To stop them.
To call them back.
To explain.
To hold on.

But no words came.

Because at that moment, nothing else mattered.

The woman he had loved — the only one he had
ever truly loved — was gone.

And with her went the last fragile hope of
forgiveness, of returning, of fixing what had been
shattered.

There was no next time now.
No day to apologize.
No chance to say "I'm sorry."

All that was left was the silence.

And the man who had to live inside it.

When Lerato walked past him with the children, the door clicked softly behind them.

The silence that followed was not the same silence that had lived in the house before.
This one was final.
Heavy.
True.

Mosa remained seated in the same chair, unmoving, staring at the floor.

And that is when it hit him.

Lerato was not Dimakatso.
She never had been.
She never could be.

He had tried to make her fill a space that was not hers.
Tried to shape their home in the image of the one he had destroyed.
But all this time, he had been living in a shadow — loving a memory while standing beside a living woman who wanted him, who tried to reach him, who finally realized she never stood a chance against a ghost.

And the children...

He had named them Bokang and Dineo, hoping
the names would bring back what had been lost.
But names were not souls.
Children are not replacements.
Love cannot be copied.

He saw it now.

The real Bokang was gone.
The real Dineo was somewhere far away, growing
up without him.
And now the real Dimakatso was gone too — not
just out of his reach,
but out of this world.

The woman who had loved him when he had
nothing,
the woman who had stood beside him through
laughter and through hunger,
the woman who had given him children and a
home,
the woman who had waited, silently, for just one
word...

That woman was gone.

And he had never said it.

Not once.

He felt the weight of the truth settle in his chest
— cold, heavy, merciless:

No one can replace what you lose through pride.
Some things, once broken, never return.
And some apologies, once delayed, come too late.

Mosa bowed his head.
His hands shook.
His breath broke in his throat.

For the first time since the night he lost his son —
he cried.

Not loudly.
Not violently.

But silently —
deep, slow tears
from a place far inside the soul,
where regret burns forever.

Chapter 10: The Door He Feared to Knock

The news of Dimakatso's funeral spread quickly, but the moment Mosa heard, his body went cold.

He could not go.
He wanted to.
He wanted to run, fall at her coffin, and beg for forgiveness that was now forever out of reach.

But he knew he had no right to stand beside her.

So he sent his family instead — sisters, cousins, nephews — to pay respects on his behalf.
They arrived with flowers, blankets, offerings, and respectful silence.

The yard was full of mourners.
People who had loved Dimakatso.
People who remembered Mosa and Dimakatso as they once were.

And then the crowd parted.

Dineo walked in.

She was grown now.
A nurse.
Graceful, confident, composed — just like her
mother.
Her posture, her kindness, her eyes — a mirror of
Dimakatso.

Even grief could not make her small.

She greeted relatives gently.
She accepted condolences with maturity beyond
her age.
She thanked Mosa's family sincerely — she held
no bitterness toward them.
She hugged them, sat with them, allowed them to
mourn with her.

But she did not ask about Mosa.
She did not speak his name.

Her heart had learned to survive without him.

Mosa was there.
But not among them.

He stood far, very far, behind a tall acacia tree
beyond the gate —
where no one would turn and see him.

He watched the coffin being lowered into the ground.

He watched his daughter wipe her mother's grave marker with her hand.
He watched her shoulders shake as she cried quietly — not loudly, not dramatically — but with the kind of pain that lives deep and forever.

He pressed his knuckles against his mouth to stop himself from making a sound.

His knees nearly gave out.

But he stayed silent.

Unseen.
Unheard.
Unwelcome — and knowing it.

That day changed him entirely.

When he got home, he called his lawyer.

"Bring me the box."

The lawyer arrived in the evening, holding the
same wooden box that had once lived in the back
of Mosa's wardrobe.
The one filled with:

- The family pictures
- The unsent letters
- The marriage certificate

Mosa held the box to his chest as though it were
something living.

Then, slowly, he returned the pictures to the
walls.

One by one.

The house looked like it used to.

But the laughter was gone.

The warmth was gone.

The family was gone.

Only memories remained.

Chapter 11: The Quiet Years

Time did what time always does — it moved
forward, whether hearts were ready or not.

The seasons rolled through the farm like tides.
Summer heat baking the soil.
Winter frost whitening the grass.
Rain coming and going without permission.

And Mosa moved through those years like a
shadow.

He woke early, fed the pigs, walked the land, and
returned to silence.
The house remained neat — curtains washed,
floors swept, beds made — as though at any
moment the door might open and life would
return.
But it didn't.

His body grew older.
His shoulders curved inward.
His hands developed a slight tremor, especially
when the mornings were cold.

But his mind remained sharp — sharp enough to
remember everything.

And then one morning, he did something he had not done since the day of the funeral.

He drove to the cemetery.

He walked slowly, holding flowers in one hand and a folded letter in the other.

He knew exactly where the grave was — he had never forgotten.
How could he?

He stood before the headstone:

Dimakatso Marutle
Beloved daughter, mother, and wife.

His chest tightened.

He knelt — slowly, carefully — as though kneeling before something holy.

He opened the letter.

And he read aloud.

His voice was soft, cracked, uneven — but steady:

"My wife...
I was wrong.
I should have listened.
I should have stopped.
I should have said I was sorry.
I should have chosen love over pride."

His breath shook.

He continued anyway.

"You were the best thing that ever happened to
me.
I did not deserve you.
I still don't."

When he finished, he folded the letter with
trembling hands, and tucked it carefully into the
flowerpot beside her name.

Then he placed the flowers.

He touched the headstone — with the gentleness
of a man touching memory.

Then he left.

He returned the next day.
And the next.
And the next.

Every day, he brought:
• Fresh flowers
• One letter

He would read the letter aloud — sometimes whispering through tears he didn't bother wiping — then tuck it into the flowerpot and go.

The cemetery groundskeepers never moved the letters.
They began to recognize him — the quiet farmer who came with flowers and sorrow.
They learned to leave the flowerpot undisturbed.

Soon, the pot was filled — carefully stacked, folded letters of apology, love, memory, regret.
Some had dried from rain.
Some had softened from weather.
But he continued.

His apology — slow, daily, endless — was the only conversation he had left.

Meanwhile, Dineo lived.

She built a career.
She healed others.
She carried her mother's grace and her father's
strength.

She visited her mother's grave too — though not
every day.
But when she came, she saw the flowers.
And the letters.

She never read them.
She didn't touch them.

She knew who they were from.

And sometimes she cried.
Not out of anger.
Not out of longing.

But because love is complicated.

She loved her father.
She also stayed away from him.
Both were true.

And neither cancelled the other.

Mosa continued aging quietly.

He no longer stood tall.
His steps grew slower.
His breath heavier.
But still — every day — he went to her.

Reading.
Remembering.
Regretting.

Not because he believed she could hear him.

But because it was all he had left to give.

Chapter 12: The Words Too Long Unspoken

Time did not take Mosa suddenly.
It softened him first.

His steps grew slower, his shoulders lighter, his
voice quieter.
There was no illness, no doctor's diagnosis — just
a man who knew in his bones that the journey was
almost over, and he was tired.

Tired of regret.
Tired of silence.
Tired of carrying love like a wound.

He wanted to rest — to join Dimakatso and
Bokang where time could not follow.

But before he left, he had to make something
right.

He had to call Dineo — his first daughter.
And he had to call Lerato and the children he had
tried to rebuild his world with.

Not to erase the past.
But to finally speak the truth.

He called Lerato first.
She did not answer.

Days passed.

He called again.

Still silence.

He did not blame her.

_____

One afternoon, Lerato visited Dimakatso's grave.

She brought flowers, as she sometimes did — out of love and respect.

That is when she saw it:

The flowerpot.
Full.
Overflowing.

Dozens of letters.

She knew who wrote them.

She lifted one carefully.
The paper was softened by rain, wrinkled by time.

She read.

Every apology.
Every memory.
Every admission of guilt.
Every I should have listened.
Every I loved you.
Every I failed you.
Every I am sorry.

Tears fell onto the paper.

Not for a man she once loved.

But for a man who had finally learned how to love too late.

She went home, sat quietly for a long while, then picked up her phone.

She didn't call Mosa.

She called her uncle.

"Tell him... tell him I will come."

On the morning of the visit, Dineo (the first daughter) arrived at the farm at the same time as Lerato and her children.

There was hesitation at first — quiet recognition, quiet surprise.
No anger.
Just life, showing how it had unfolded differently for each of them.

Mosa stood on the porch when they approached.

His voice trembled.

He looked at his daughter — the first one.

For a moment, no words came.

Time paused between them.

Then the smallest, simplest word broke the silence — the word he had spent a lifetime unable to say:

"Dineo... I'm sorry."

Her breath caught.

Her eyes lifted.

She had never expected to hear it.
Not from him.
Not in this lifetime.

And before she could speak, his voice cracked:

"I was wrong.
I was proud.
I hurt you.
I hurt us all.
I wish... I wish I could go back."

Her breath caught.

She had never heard those words from him.
Not once.

She stepped forward.

"I forgive you, Papa."

Not because it erased anything.
But because she needed to stop bleeding from old wounds.

She hugged him — and he wept into her shoulder.

————

Then he turned to Lerato.

His voice broke.

"Lerato... I am sorry.
I brought you into a wound I never healed.
I tried to turn you into someone you could never be.
I was unfair to you, and to your children.
You deserved love I did not know how to give."

Lerato nodded — soft, steady, dignified.

"I forgave you a long time ago, Mosa."

And she meant it.

Her children stood beside her.

Mosa knelt slightly — his age making the motion slow — and looked at them.

"Bokang... Dineo... you do not carry the sins of my past.
You are your own lives.
Your own futures.
I am sorry for trying to make you memories."

The two young adults looked at one another, then at him — and stepped forward to embrace him.

———

Mosa stood, wiped his eyes, and said — with a small, trembling smile:

"Dineo... meet Dineo."

And the two girls laughed — a soft, warm laugh that broke something open in the air.

They hugged — sister to sister, not by blood, but by story.

Bokang smiled too — the kind of smile that belongs to healing.

And for the first time in decades,
the house felt warm again.

Not perfect.
Not restored.

But peaceful.

Just peaceful.

That night, when everyone had left, Mosa sat alone on the porch, watching the sun slide behind the hills.

For the first time in decades, his heart felt light.

He whispered into the evening air:

"I fixed what I could.
I'll rest soon.
I'm coming, Dimakatso."

And the wind moved softly through the trees —

as if answering.

Chapter 13: Pride Before a Fall

The farm had grown quiet over the years — but it was no longer a lonely quiet.
It was a peaceful one.

After the reunion, Dineo visited often.
Sometimes alone, sometimes with her husband, sometimes with her children.
Lerato visited too, now and then — always warmly, always respectfully.

And Mosa, who once had nothing but silence, now had voices in the house again.

One late afternoon, Dineo called:

"Papa, we're all coming for dinner tonight."

"All?" he asked.

She laughed softly.

"Yes. My family. And... them too."

She meant Lerato, Bokang, and the second Dineo.

Mosa closed his eyes and nodded.

"I'll be ready."

That Evening

The house smelled of warm stew and baked
bread.
Dineo (the younger one) and Dineo (the older
one) teased each other in the kitchen while
preparing the dishes.
Bokang helped set the table.
Children played in the yard, laughing — the sound
carrying through the air like something returned
from long ago.

Lerato arrived with her husband — gentle, kind,
steady —
a man who loved her the way she had always
deserved.

There was no awkwardness.
No tension.
No pain.

Just people.
Trying.
Living.

Mosa sat at the head of the table.

It was the first time in decades that every seat was full.

He looked around slowly:

- His daughter — the first Dineo, now a woman of strength and grace.
- Her husband — respectful, steady.
- Their children — bright-eyed, curious, the future itself.
- Bokang — no longer a shadow of the past, but his own person.
- The second Dineo — smiling, confident, warm.
- Lerato — healed, whole, with someone who loved her fully.

He felt something he had not felt in so long: full.

They ate.
They talked.
They laughed.

Not loudly.
Not excitedly.

But gently.
The way a wound closes — little by little — without needing to be spoken about.

Later, when everyone was leaving, the eldest Dineo whispered as she hugged him:

"I'm glad we came back, Papa."

Mosa closed his eyes and held her tight.

"Me too, ngwanake. Me too."

The weeks after the reunion were quiet — the soft kind of quiet, the peaceful kind.
The farm felt different now.
Not full again, no — but warmer.
As if the house had exhaled after holding its breath for years.

Mosa woke early each morning, like he always had.
He still made his tea.
He still walked the land.
He still visited the pigs — his old friends who had grown grey around the ears, just like him.

But something in him was lighter.

He no longer avoided the rooms with the photographs.
He didn't keep his eyes down when he passed Bokang's bicycle or Dineo's little chair.
He could look — and remember — and not break.

He had said what he needed to say.
And he had been heard.

One afternoon, he stood at the kitchen window —
the same one where Dimakatso once used to
stand and watch him walk down to the tractors.

He smiled.

Not with sadness.
Not with longing.

But with gratitude.

He whispered her name — softly, reverently:

"Dima."

Then he closed his eyes, and in the quiet, he felt
her.

Not like a ghost.
Not like a memory.
But like peace.

That evening, he sat on the porch just as the sun
dipped behind the hills.
The sky glowed warm orange — the exact shade of
the days when life was simple and full.

And that was where Dineo found him.

She had brought him dinner — pap, beef stew, and the cabbage with carrots her mother used to make.

"Papa?" she called softly.

He didn't answer.

He sat in his wooden chair, head resting slightly to the side, eyes closed — as though he had simply drifted into sleep.

Dineo smiled — ready to tease him for dozing off — but when she touched his shoulder, his hand slipped gently from his lap.

There was no tension in his face.
No strain.
No fear.

Just peace.

He had gone quietly.

As if walking into another room.

As if going to meet the two people he had been calling for all these years.

Dimakatso.
Bokang.

Dineo placed her hand over his and closed her eyes.

There were tears — yes — but they were soft tears.
Not sharp.
Not tearing.

Tears of love for a father who finally tried, even when it was late.

She whispered:

"Rest, Papa.
I'll be okay now."

The funeral was small — dignified.
Not loud with grief — but full of understanding.

Lerato came with her husband and her children.
They stood beside Dineo, one Dineo's hand in the other's.
Bokang stood tall, quiet, respectful — the way the first Bokang
would have.

Mosa's family came too — not as a crowd this time — but as a
circle.

No enemies.
No bitterness.

Just people who had finally laid down what was too heavy to
carry.

———

When the coffin was lowered, Dineo stepped forward and
placed one of her father's letters — the ones he had written to
her but could never send — on top of it.

She whispered:

"Rest, Papa.
I'll be okay now."

Final Message

Pride does not roar.
It does not shout.
It does not announce itself.

It arrives quietly —
in the pauses where apology should be.

It builds slowly —
in the spaces where love should speak.

And in the end,
it steals the one thing
you never get back:

Time.

But forgiveness, though slow,
though painful,
though imperfect—

is still possible.

Even late.

Even at the end.

And that is why this story is told.

So that those who read it
will not wait too long
to say the words that heal:

"I'm sorry."

This is the story of a father who loved too late,
a mother torn between love and pain,
and a daughter who learned that forgiveness is
not forgetting —
it is choosing to no longer bleed.

A deeply human tale about love and regret,
about silence that destroys,
and the cost of waiting too long to say "I'm sorry."

Sometimes the lesson is learned only when it is
too late.
Sometimes the fall teaches more than the pride
ever did.

About the Author

Thuli Marutle Leigh writes with honesty, empathy,
and emotional depth.
Her work speaks to anyone who has loved deeply,
lost painfully, or struggled with words left unsaid.
She explores the bonds that hold families
together — and the silences that pull them apart.
Her stories do not just entertain—
they teach, soften, and restore what is often left
unspoken.

This is the story of a father who loved too late,
a mother torn between love and pain,
and a daughter who learned that forgiveness is
not forgetting —
it is choosing to no longer bleed.

A deeply human tale about love and regret,
about silence that destroys,
and the cost of waiting too long to say "I'm sorry."

Sometimes the lesson is learned only when it is
too late.
Sometimes the fall teaches more than the pride
ever did.

About the Author

Thuli Marutle Leigh writes with honesty, empathy,
and emotional depth.
Her work speaks to anyone who has loved deeply,
lost painfully, or struggled with words left unsaid.
She explores the bonds that hold families
together — and the silences that pull them apart.
Her stories do not just entertain—
they teach, soften, and restore what is often left
unspoken.